Chicken Socks

and other contagious poems

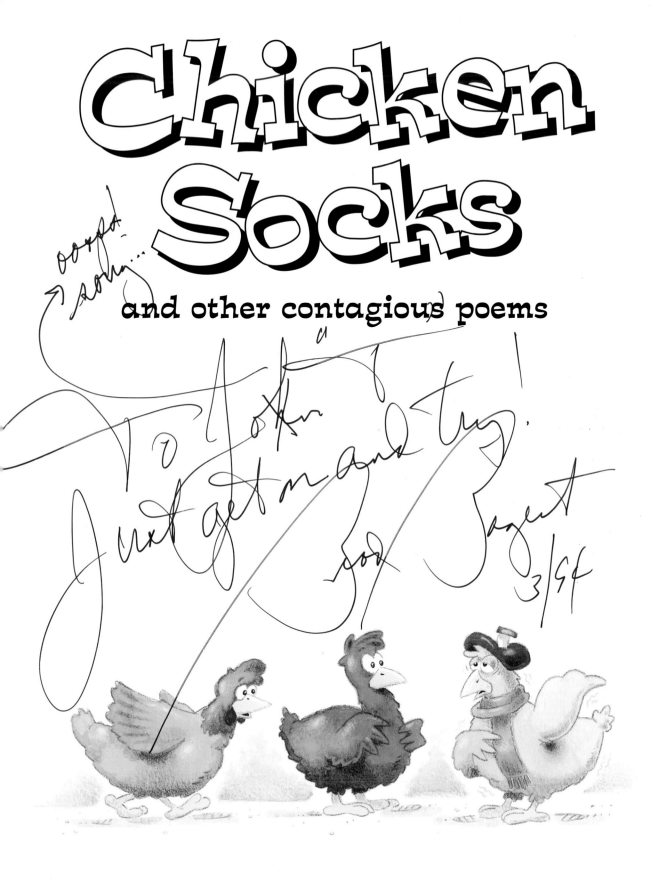

oorpd? roby...

To John

Just get on and try.

God Bless!

Baggett 3/94

Chicken Socks

and other contagious poems

by Brod Bagert
Illustrations by Tim Ellis

To my dad, Ben Bagert Sr.,
who taught me to work,
who taught me to persevere,
and who never missed a Little League game
—B.B.

To my loving wife, Laura, and
our new daughter, Hailey
—T.E.

Text copyright © 1993 by Brod Bagert
Illustrations copyright © 1993 by Boyds Mills Press

Published by Wordsong
Boyds Mills Press, Inc.
A Highlights Company
815 Church Street
Honesdale, Pennsylvania 18431
Printed in Mexico

Publisher Cataloging-in-Publication Data
Bagert, Brod.
    Chicken socks and other contagious poems / by Brod Bagert ;
illustrations by Tim Ellis.—1st ed.
    p. : col. ill. ; cm.
Summary : A collection of humorous poems about school, behavior,
learning to ride a bike, and more.
ISBN 1-56397-292-1
1. Humorous poetry, American—Juvenile literature. 2. Children's poetry, American. (1.
Humorous Poetry. 2. American poetry.) I. Ellis, Tim, ill.
II. Title.
811.54—dc20   1993   CIP
Library of Congress Catalog Card Number 93-60474

First edition, 1993
Book designed by Tim Gillner
The text of this book is set in 14-point Avant Garde.
The illustrations are done in watercolors and colored pencils.
Distributed by St. Martin's Press

10 9 8 7 6 5 4 3 2

Contents

Contagious

Shut the windows,
Lock the locks,
Gretchen's got the chicken socks.

So contagious,
It's outrageous,
She's really got the blues.
I guess we should be glad
She didn't catch the chicken shoes.

The Stupid Lie

It really hurt my feelings
When she didn't say good-bye,
But this wet stuff on my face
Is from dirt caught in my eye—
Cuz boys are rough
And boys are tough
And boys don't ever cry.

I know it looks like real tears,
But you know I'd never try
To fool you guys by making up
Some kind of stupid lie—
Cuz boys are rough
And boys are tough
And boys don't ever cry.

Even if I want to cry
I know I never should,
But sometimes—when it hurts real bad—
Sometimes I wish I could—
But boys are rough
And boys are tough
And boys can never never
Never ever cry.

Split Pants

I did a handspring on the ground
And heard that awful tearing sound.

The girls began to giggle—
Tee hee hee!

The boys all laughed and jeered—
Na haaa!

So I held my ears,
And closed my eyes,
And **POOF**—I disappeared!

The Worm Song

Worms for breakfast
Worms for lunch
Worms for supper too,
Worms for Mom
Worms for Dad
And worms for me and you.

I cannot eat another worm
Please give me something new.
My stomach is real hungry
For a bowl of lizard stew.

Next Week's Angel

Monday night I fibbed to Mom.

Tuesday I was better.

Wednesday I slipped up again,
I read my sister's letter.
It was mushy muck and lovey talk
And smoochy goo,
What fun . . . until she caught me
And whacked me with her shoe.

Thursday I played after dark.

Friday was a bummer.
I filled the toilet with red paint
And flushed it on the plumber.

Saturday I was doing fine
Until Nathan P. MacNagg
Made me put my grass snake
In his mama's grocery bag.

But now it's Sunday morning
And I feel a little sad
As I get down on my knees in church—
How could I be so bad?

I promise next week I'll be good,
I'll be everything I ain't.
Yeah, by this time next Sunday
I'll be shining like a saint.

If You Love Me

Give me candy, Mama.
A little candy if you care.
I just don't want a carrot,
Or an apple or a pear.
I need chocolate-covered caramel
With cookies—layer on layer.
A little candy if you love me,
Give me candy if you care.

The 57-Pound Rodeo Kid

When I ride my horse
I show him who's boss.

I turn him to the left!
I turn him to the right!
I run him up the middle!

I'm glad that big horse doesn't know
His rider is so little.

The Bad-Mood Bug

I don't know what I want today
But nothing feels quite right.
If I had an ice-cream pie
I wouldn't take a bite.

I wouldn't ride a water slide
Climb monkey bars or trees,
No games, no toys, no magic wands,
No elephants for me.

There's a grouchy bug inside me
And it's usually asleep,
But when the grumpy thing wakes up
I turn into a creep.

Progress

Great-grandpa had a gramophone
That weighed a hundred pounds;
Granddad had a hi-fi
That stood four feet off the ground;
Papa had components
Stacked in stages like a rocket:
And me . . .
I've got a Walkman
I can fit inside my pocket.

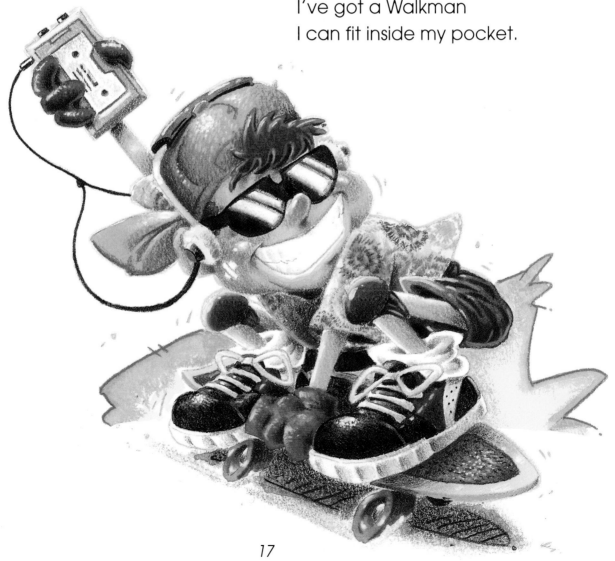

The Time I Learned to Ride My Bike

My daddy said, "Today's the day
You're going to learn to ride."
So I ran upstairs into my room
To find a place to hide.

But now I'm sitting on this bike,
No training wheels in sight.
How did he talk me into this?
I sure hope he was right.

I feel the pedals turn.
I start to move real slow.
What if I fall and hurt myself?
"Oh Daddy!
Please!
Don't let me go!"

His hands are gone—I'm doing it—
Much longer than I dared.
It's not so hard—it's kind of fun—
Now why was I so scared?

I was just great—they cheered for me—
My daddy didn't lie.
If you want to ride a bike,
You just get on and try.

Night Pictures

None of it makes sense to me.

Pegasus the Horse is shaped like a square,
Taurus the Bull is a V,
And for Leo the Lion,
A question mark
Is all that I can see.

I guess those guys
In ancient times
Who named our constellations
Were all a bunch of dreamers
With wild imaginations.

Paleontology

My sister got some college books
And in one of them I found
A picture of a dinosaur
Half-buried in the ground.

And this guy was trying to dig it up
With a tiny brush
And a teeny tiny spoon.
When bones are buried for a billion years
There's no rush to finish soon.

The First Day of Summer

7 A.M.
I rode my bike.

8 A.M.
We went swimming.

9 A.M.
I helped my dad
In the garden with his trimming.

10 A.M.
We played baseball.

12 NOON
We picnicked in the park.
We threw horseshoes
And ran races
And played games till after dark.

But now it's 8 P.M.
And it's oh so sad but true,
My summer has just started
And there's nothing left to do.

Secrets

John David had a secret
And I promised not to tell,
So he told me all about it
And I listened very well.

Now his secret is my secret
But I really want to **yell** it.
Why is it that a secret is no fun
Unless you tell it?

The Fight at Little Recess

He pushed me
In front of all my friends.
He told me I was chicken.
So I said, "That all depends."

They laughed at me, I could have died,
I was about to cry.
Oh please no tears, do something quick—
So I socked him in his eye.

We rolled and kicked and twisted arms
From the sidewalk to the grass
Until the bell began to ring—
At last! It was time for class.

He figured he could pick on me
But I sure gave him a whirl.
The fool thought I'd be scared to fight
Just cuz I'm a girl.

The Easter Kitchen

We did our best to avoid a mess,
You know we always try.
We put paper on the counter
To protect it from the dye.

We poured the water in real slow
To make sure it didn't spill,
And when we started dunking eggs
We held each egg real still.

But then we learned to make new colors
By mixin' up and switchin'
And . . .
What I'm trying to tell you, Mom,
Is that . . .
We sort of dyed the kitchen.

Final Exams

I would ride a wave
To an island of pleasure,
Or search the deep
For a chest full of treasure,
Or float alone
In a hot-air balloon
To follow the fog
All the way to the moon,
Or ride a camel
Through cold desert night,
Or walk through a forest
Lit with green fairy light.

I'm ready for life's journey
Through happiness or sorrow,
Just save me from this stupid test
I have to take tomorrow.

If Only I Could Fly

If only I could fly.
If only I were magic
I would leap into the sky,
I would soar up to the mountains
Then splash down into the sea,
I'd do loop-de-loops
Above the clouds,
How famous I would be!
And that would make me happy,
I'd never ever cry
If only only only if,
If only I could fly.

Barnyard

Goats and chickens and ducks and pigs
And sheep and geese that squawk,
The air around this barnyard smells
A lot like Noah's Ark.

Caterpillars

They ate up every plant in sight
With munchy little monster bites,
These nasty worms with legs that crawl
So creepy up the garden wall,
Green prickly fuzz to hurt and sting
Each unsuspecting living thing.
How I hate them! Oh, you know
I'd love to squish one with my toe.
But then I see past their disguise—
Someday they'll all be butterflies.

Yesterday's Magnolia

I walked outside this morning
And saw a strange man climbing in my tree.
How nice that he would like
To do the same fun things as me.

But when I heard his chain saw growl
The tears rushed down my face,
He was about to use it
To chop down my favorite place.

I yelled, "Wait!
Don't cut another branch!"
Too late.
The only tree that I could climb
And now . . . there's just a hole.

I feel so sad and angry
But I don't know who to blame.
No matter what you do in life . . .
Nothing ever stays the same.

The Thank-you Poem

Thank you for another day,
To love
To work
To worship
And to play.
Thank you for these heartbeats,
This breath,
These precious hours.
Help me give love like your sun . . .
And receive it like your flowers.